Helloooooo again!

My name's **Ty**, and I'm seven. Did you already **know** that?

If you didn't, let me **explain**.

This is a book about me and my **crazy** life!

Which involves a lot of **sisters** (TEENSY and big and **BIGGER**)

And things **flying** where they shouldn't fly and hyenas and JACKALOPES!

Okay, kidding, **no jackalopes** . . . MAYBE. HOLD YER HORSES!

You have to **turn** the page and **start** reading to find out.

THE LIFE OF TY

NON-RANDOM ACTS OF KINDNESS

BOOK 2

THE LIFE OF TY

Non-
Random
Acts of
Kindness

BOOK 2

LAUREN MYRACLE

Illustrated by Jed Henry

PUFFIN BOOKS
An Imprint of Penguin Group (USA)

PUFFIN BOOKS
Published by the Penguin Group
Penguin Group (USA) LLC
375 Hudson Street
New York, New York 10014

USA * Canada * UK * Ireland * Australia
New Zealand * India * South Africa * China

penguin.com
A Penguin Random House Company

First published in the United States of America by Dutton Children's Books,
an imprint of Penguin Group (USA) LLC, 2014
Published by Puffin Books, an imprint of Penguin Young Readers Group, 2015

THE LIBRARY OF CONGRESS HAS CATALOGED THE DUTTON CHILDREN'S BOOKS EDITION AS FOLLOWS:
Myracle, Lauren, date.
The life of Ty : non-random acts of kindness / Lauren Myracle ;
illustrated by Jed Henry.
pages cm.
Summary: "In the second book of the series, seven-year-old Ty Perry
discovers that being kind is part of being Ty"—Provided by publisher.
ISBN 978-0-525-42266-2 (hardback)
[1. Kindness—Fiction. 2. Schools—Fiction. 3. Brothers and sisters—Fiction.]
I. Henry, Jed, illustrator. II Title. III. Title: Non-random acts of kindness.
PZ7.M9955Lhn 2014
[Fic]—dc23   2013032576

Puffin Books ISBN 978-0-14-242319-6

Printed in the United States of America

Designed by Irene Vandervoort

1 3 5 7 9 10 8 6 4 2

To Mirabelle, who cartwheels
through life, spreading kindness
wherever she goes

THE LIFE OF TY

NON-RANDOM ACTS OF KINDNESS

BOOK 2

CHAPTER ONE

Today, my big sister Winnie tells me I have crazy-boy hair. My bigger sister, Sandra, pulls into the drop-off lane at Trinity, where I go to school, and glances back at me. She says, "Whoa, dude, it *is*. Did you stick your finger in an electrical outlet?"

"No," I say huffily. I am not the sort of person who would stick his finger into an electrical outlet, and my sisters know it. Except then I imagine what it would be like if I *did* stick my finger into an outlet. Would it mainly hurt and be only a little bit interesting, or would it be mainly interesting and only hurt a little?

Would it really make my hair go crazy?

But *how*, exactly, would I wedge my finger into

an electrical outlet? I'd have to take off the out-let cover. I'd have to use a screwdriver. I do like screwdrivers. I microwaved one once by accident, and it popped and made sparks, and Mom ran over and said, "Ty! What in heaven's name? No. *No* microwaving hand tools. Understood?"

Hmm. Maybe I *am* the sort of boy who would stick his finger into an electrical outlet. Also, it *might* not have been an accident. With the microwave and the screwdriver. But not totally on purpose either?

"Here," Winnie says, digging a hairbrush out of her backpack and tossing it to me. When San-

dra drives me to school, she and Winnie always get to sit in the front, and I always get stuck in the back, because I'm seven and so that means I'm short(ish) and so that's the law.

At least I don't have to sit in a car seat anymore. My third sister, who is only one month old and named Maggie, sits in a car seat. It's a cute car seat. It has jungle animals all over it. Even so, it smells like dangerous milk.

"Brush your hair and skedaddle," Sandra says. "Winnie and I need to get to school, too."

I drag Winnie's brush through my hair. Sandra and Winnie watch.

"Stop staring at me," I say.

"But you're so cute," Winnie says.

"And funny looking," Sandra says.

"You're making me feel like a monkey," I say. "Like a monkey at the zoo, and I'm in a cage, and you two are outside the cage, just staring and staring."

"That's how it works at zoos," Sandra says.

"Hey, do you think Mom would let me get a monkey?" I ask. "And I could give it to Teensy Baby Maggie?"

Sandra's laugh bubbles over with delight. "Um, let me think. *No.*"

Winnie cocks her head. "Why would you give the monkey to Maggie?"

"Because I promised," I say. I squirm. "I promised Maggie I'd get her a pet, because of . . . you know."

At first she doesn't. Then she does. "Ahhh," Winnie says. "Because of Pingy, the penguin you stole from the Georgia Aquarium."

"Borrowed!" I say. "Not stole!"

"Ty Perry, penguin thief," Sandra says. She clucks. "Second grader by day, hardened criminal by night."

I pinch the underside of my leg, and guess what? I'm not *hard.* I'm squishy. Plus, Sandra and Winnie snuck Pingy the penguin back to the aquarium when no one was watching. He's back with his mommy penguin and his brother and sister penguins now.

My brain knows that's good. My heart still misses him.

The car behind us edges out of line and pulls away. Another car takes its place. Kids push through the heavy glass doors of the school and are gobbled up by the building.

"Ty, we're blocking traffic," Sandra says.

I give Winnie her hairbrush. I open the car door and plant one foot on the asphalt.

"Have a good day," Winnie says. "And don't worry about Teensy Baby Maggie. I think she's more interested in flopping her arms around than in getting a pet."

I plant my other foot on the asphalt. I climb out of the car.

"Anyway," Winnie goes on, "are you forgetting about Sweetie-Pie?"

My eyebrows shoot up. "Sweetie-Pie is a *cat*. *Your* cat."

"Well, technically. But I can share."

Sharing a pet sounds about as fun as sharing a marshmallow. Someone always gets more. Plus, sometimes Sweetie-Pie scratches. Sometimes Sweetie-Pie hides under the sofa and then leaps out and nips my ankles.

Maggie needs a better pet than Sweetie-Pie, and it needs to be her own.

Sandra clears her throat, which is code for, *And now good-bye, and close the door or I'll zoom off with it open—and who knows how many children will be knocked to the ground like bowling pins?*

I shut the door, and my sisters drive away.

During morning meeting, Mrs. Webber tells us about an exciting project we'll be working on this week. She's the one who uses the word "exciting." The project is that we all have to do a random act of kindness, because that's what it says on the bumper sticker she shows us: *Practice Random Acts of Kindness*. Then, on Friday, we'll stand up one by one and say what we did. She tells us that part's called a *recitation*.

Taylor raises his hand. "Why?" he asks, without waiting to be called on.

"Well, because that's what it's called," Mrs. Webber says. She's sitting in her swivel chair, which she's rolled to the center of the room. We're sitting on the carpet in front of her.

"But *why?*" Taylor says.

"Because the word 'recitation' is related to the word 'recite,' and it's important to know how to recite things—like reports and homework—in front of a crowd. The best way to learn is by practicing."

"YES, BUT WHY?" Taylor says. Taylor has no problem speaking in front of a crowd. He sometimes has a problem *not* speaking in front of a crowd. When that happens, Mrs. Webber sets an egg timer for five minutes and gives it to him.

I have never been given the egg timer, and I plan to keep it that way. Just imagining it gives me the shivers.

Breezie, who likes to wear dresses, raises her hand. She wiggles it.

"Yes, Breezie?" Mrs. Webber says.

"He means why do we have to do random acts of kindness," Breezie explains.

"Oh," Mrs. Webber says. She crosses one leg over the other and swings her top foot back and forth. "Well, because we are one big human family, and kindness is important."

Taylor's hand shoots back up. He says, "But why do we have to *practice* them?"

"Practice them?" Mrs. Webber says. "No, that's just what it says on the bumper sticker. To *practice* random acts of kindness just means to *do* random acts of kindness."

I raise my hand. I don't wave it all around.

"Yes, Ty?"

"Are our kindnesses supposed to be on purpose?"

"I'm sorry?"

"Um, apology accepted."

"No, I mean . . . what?"

"Oh. Well, how can we do random acts of kindness on purpose?" I say. "If they're random, they're not on purpose. If they're on purpose, how can they be random?"

Other kids nod.

"Yeah," Elizabeth says. "They can't be both."

First Mrs. Webber frowns, and then she frowns even deeper, and then she lets go of her frown altogether. "You're right, Ty," she says. "Tell you what, let's change it to *non*-random acts of kindness."

"Okay," I say, and I'm proud of her for listening, which grown-ups don't always do. Especially when they're wrong.

Lexie, who is sometimes my best friend and sometimes Breezie's best friend, thrusts her hand into the air.

"Yes, Lexie?"

"I like your clogs," Lexie says. "Are they made of wood?"

Mrs. Webber leans forward and squints at them. "Why, yes. Yes, they are."

"They're pretty," Lexie says.

"Thank you. Did you have a question about the recitation?"

Lexie folds her hands in her lap. Her legs are crisscross applesauce, and she smiles sweetly. "Nope, I'm good."

Mrs. Webber scans the rest of us. Her hair is already coming loose from the way she's pinned it up. "Any other questions?" she asks. Like Lexie, she smiles sweetly, but her tone reminds me of Mom when it's almost dinnertime and Teensy Baby Maggie is crying and the spaghetti is boiling so much that sploshes of water leap from the pot and sizzle on the stove.

I think of Mrs. Webber's coffee mug, which says IS IT FRIDAY YET?

"No?" Mrs. Webber says. "Fabulous. In that case, let's get started with our small group math." She stands up quickly—*too* quickly—and her chair scoots backward. Her eyes widen and her arms spin like pinwheels.

Uh-oh.

She falls smack on her bottom, and her legs swoop up, and one of her wooden clogs flies off her foot.

"*Ow!*" Lexie cries. She doubles over and rocks back and forth. "*Ow, ow, owwie, ow!*"

"Lexie!" Breezie says. "Are you all right?"

"That was *awesome!*" Taylor says.

Lexie clutches her head. "*Owww!*"

Mrs. Webber pushes herself to a sitting position. Her dazed eyes move around and land on me.

"Ty?"

I gulp. "Yes?"

"Would you please get Mrs. Jacobs?" Mrs. Jacobs is Trinity's assistant principal. She dresses like a lady police officer, but she's nice.

I scramble up. "Uh-huh. I mean, okay. I mean yes!"

Mrs. Webber's clog is on the floor right next to me. It must have hit Lexie's head and then bounced off, and now it's next to me, and guess what else? It's also next to an electrical outlet, which is staring at me from the wall. *A real live electrical outlet.* I grab the clog quickly, because it looks creepy just lying there. And I *don't* want to stick my finger into an electrical outlet, and I don't want anyone else to, either.

I go to Mrs. Webber and hold out her clog. She takes it. For a moment, I'm frozen, and then I dash to get help.

CHAPTER TWO

Lexie has to leave school early and go home, even though it's the beginning of the day.

"Oh, my poor girl," her mom says when she walks into Mrs. Webber's classroom. We've settled Lexie in a beanbag in the reading nook. Breezie's holding a frozen sponge from the office against Lexie's forehead, and Hannah is rubbing Lexie's feet. (She gently took off Lexie's shoes first and placed them to the side. Sparkly black high-tops with rubber soles. No wood.)

Elizabeth and I are guarding Lexie from Taylor, who's singing a rap song for her that involves dancing. His rap is okay, but his dance is on the wild side.

"Hi, Mom," Lexie says.

Hannah lets go of Lexie's foot and takes Lexie's hand, which she pats. "See? Your mom's here now. You'll be fine."

Lexie rolls her eyes. "I'm not a baby," she says. "I got beaned by a flying clog, that's all."

Mrs. Webber rises from her big teacher's desk, and she and Lexie's mother join us in the reading nook.

"Charlene, I am *so* sorry," she says. "Taylor, this is not the time for dancing."

"Susan, please," Lexie's mom tells Mrs. Webber. "You didn't kick her on purpose. I know that."

"I didn't *kick* her at all," Mrs. Webber says. "Did someone tell you I kicked her?"

"It wasn't my fault either," Lexie says. "I was just sitting there being good. Right, Mrs. Webber?"

"Absolutely," Mrs. Webber says, while at the same time Lexie's mom cries, "Of course, sweetie! Accidents happen to everyone." She pushes past Taylor and helps Lexie to her feet. "Let's swing you by the Youth Clinic *just in case*, and then we'll get you home."

"Can I watch TV?" Lexie says.

"As much as you want."

"And have popsicles?"

"Lexie could live on popsicles," Lexie's mom says to us with a laugh. She takes over the job of holding Lexie's ice pack in place, and we walk as a group across the room.

Hannah gets jostled. She scowls at Chase and whispers, "Move! You're crowding me!"

"You're crowding *me*!" Chase says back.

"I'm sure Lexie's fine," Mrs. Webber says over their bickering. "But do call and let us know."

"If I have brain damage, can I skip my spelling homework?" Lexie asks.

"Brain damage?" Taylor says. He darts from one side of our procession to the other, trying to worm into the center. "Oh, man, that would be *so* epic."

"I know, right?" Lexie says.

"It would not be epic in the slightest," Mrs. Webber says. "And, Lexie, good heavens. You do not have brain damage."

Lexie shrugs. "You never know about me."

Lexie's mom laughs, which I don't approve of. I don't think Mrs. Webber does, either, because she gives Lexie's mom a funny look.

"Well, we're off," Lexie's mom says. She flashes a smile with lots of white teeth. "Lexie? Can you say bye to your friends?"

"Bye to my friends," Lexie says. *"Hopefully* I'll be back tomorrow. *Hopefully* I'll remember your names. But maybe you should wear name tags, just in case?"

"I'll make sure everyone does," Hannah says, still holding fast to Lexie's hand.

Lexie's mom pries off Hannah's fingers. "Let go now. You need to let me take Lexie with me."

"Wait!" I cry. Lexie's high-tops. The cool black sparkly ones. It occurs to me that I would really like to have a pair of black high-tops like those. Then it occurs to me that it is time for me to stay on task, so I go back to the beanbag, grab Lexie's shoes, and thrust them at Lexie's mom. "Here."

In my whole life, I hardly ever give people shoes. Today I've done it twice in one hour.

Morning recess feels strange. I file outside with the rest of the kids, but who am I supposed to play with?

In the olden days, I would have played with Joseph, who is my true best friend. But Joseph's in the hospital. He has leukemia.

He won't be in the hospital *forever,* and he's going to be okay, but he isn't here on the playground with me. That's my point.

In the newen days, I usually play with Lexie— but Lexie went home.

Sometimes I play with Taylor, but Taylor is rough. There's been enough roughness today already.

I sit under the play structure and sift through the sand and the rocks. I look up through the metal slats of the bouncy bridge. I gaze at bits of clouds. I fill my lungs up with air, then let it out in a *whoosh*.

"Can I come in?" a person asks. It's a girl person, and she's leaning over and peering at me, and it's Breezie. Breezie! Her blond ponytail is perfect and shiny and swings back and forth. I wouldn't mind touching it. I push my hands beneath me and sit on them.

She squats and duck-walks into the space under the bouncy bridge. I'm surprised, because she is not a duck-walking girl. She sits, carefully tucking her legs beneath her and fluffing out her skirt.

"It's weird without Lexie here," she says.

"I know."

"Do you think she's going to be all right?"

"I think she's *already* all right. She just has a bump on her head."

"More like a dent."

"Okay, a dent."

"Do you think it will pop back out?"

"The dent? I think so."

"Are you sure?"

No. But Breezie's eyebrows are scared, scrunchy caterpillars, so I say, "Uh-huh. I'm one hundred percent sure, that's how sure I am."

The worry leaves her face, and my heart swells, because *I* did that. I made Breezie feel better.

"Good," she says. She's silent for a few seconds. Her hand hovers over the pile of pebbles I made, and I want to say, *Go on. You're allowed.*

She pulls back her hand. She says, "Also, Taylor caught a fly."

I crane forward and peek out from beneath the bouncy bridge. I see Taylor. I see kids gathered around him.

"I think you better go over there," Breezie says.

"Me? Why?"

"Because he's Taylor, and you're . . . *not*. Please?"

Well. I crawl out from beneath the play structure and brush myself off. Reluctantly, I approach Taylor. Breezie follows, staying about ten feet behind.

"Taylor caught a fly!" Chase exclaims when he sees me. "He caught a fly, and now he's going to pull its wings off!"

"Maybe," Taylor says. His hands are cupped around something, and the something is buzzing. "Or maybe I'll eat it. Or both!"

"Taylor, no," I say. "If you have a fly in there"—I nod at his hands—"you have to let it go."

"My cousin says flies taste like carpet," Taylor
says.

"Well, he's wrong," I say.

"How do you know?"

"Because I do. Because I asked a fly once, and
he said that flies taste like . . . like . . ."

Taylor squints. He's deciding whether to pop
the fly into his mouth, I just know it.

"Like cheese puffs!" I say. "*Yucky* cheese puffs.
And the fly you caught?" I step forward and put
my ear next to Taylor's cupped hands. "*Ohhh,*" I
say. "What? What? Oh. Okay, sure."

I straighten up. "He says his name is Cheesehead. Cheesehead the Fly. So you can't eat him,
because he has a name."

Taylor doesn't know if he should believe me.

"You can't pull his wings off, either," I say.
"He's already used his special fly radar to tell all
of his fly brothers and sisters that he's trapped in
your hands, and if you hurt him, they'll come and

find you." I widen my eyes. "It will happen when you're least expecting it."

"It's true," Breezie says. She's not ten feet behind me anymore.

"But if you let him go, he'll be your special fly protector forever," I say.

"Like a fly bodyguard?" Taylor says.

"Ex*act*ly like a fly bodyguard," I say. "Only so sneaky you'll hardly even know he's there."

Taylor uncups his hands. The fly zips away. Everyone watches, and then Taylor says, "Let's play soccer. I call goalie!"

He and some other kids run to get a ball. Chase heads for the grassy field, while Hannah and Elizabeth wander toward the swing set.

"Thanks," Breezie says.

"You're welcome," I say.

We look at each other. I'm not sure what to do, so I hold out my hand. She hesitates, then shakes it. Then she spins on her heel and jogs toward

Hannah and Elizabeth. "Hey!" she calls. "Wait for me!"

I stand there, my arms dangling by my sides. I think about Lexie. I hope she's okay. I think about Joseph. Being in the hospital means Joseph's not all the way okay, but his doctor says he's doing a great job of getting more okay, which makes a small glow light up inside me. Still, I'm ready for him to hurry up and be every single bit okay, so that he can finally come back to school.

CHAPTER THREE

The next morning, Mom stands at the stove and makes breakfast like a good mommy. Dad has already left for work, and Sandra and Winnie are upstairs doing girl stuff, so for a few minutes it's just me and Baby Maggie at the table.

Actually, Baby Maggie isn't *at* the table. She's *on* the table, strapped into her bouncy chair.

"Now listen, I'm working hard on getting you a pet," I tell her in a low voice. "I don't want you to think I've forgotten, because I haven't. 'Kay?"

I jostle the bouncy seat, and Maggie nods. Her whole body nods—up, down, up, down.

"And we have eggs," Mom announces in a *ta-da* sort of way. "Ty-bug, will you call your sisters?"

"SISTERS!" I bellow. "EGGS!"

"COMING!" Winnie bellows back.

"Here's a thought," Mom says, coming to the table. "Next time I ask you to call your sisters, I want you to go to them and make sure you can see their eyeballs. Then, very politely, let them know that breakfast is ready. Can you do that?"

"Sure," I say. "But you asked me to *call* them, so I did."

"Next time, eyeballs," Mom says.

She spoons yummy, fluffy eggs onto my plate. While she's there, she kisses Maggie's rosy cheek, which *sometimes* I want to bite. Not because I want to hurt her! Because her cheeks are round and chubby, that's all.

But I bit my own arm once—it's a *little* round and a *little* chubby—and it wasn't the thrill of a lifetime. So whenever I think, *Mmm, me bite baby's cheek!*, I right away remind myself to think a second thought: *No bite! Yucky! Have cookie instead—or eggs!*

"At the end of the day, remind Lexie to go with you to the pickup line," Mom tells me. "I got a text from Lexie's mom this morning, and Lexie *will* be at school. That means your playdate is still on."

Since I'm chewing, I give her a thumbs-up.

"If she doesn't go home with you when Sandra and Winnie pick you up, she won't get to go home at all," Mom says. "So it's important she sticks with you."

I swallow. "Well, someone would pick her up *eventually*."

"I mean it, Ty," Mom insists. "Don't forget."

But Lexie doesn't let me remind her, because she's too busy being a rock star. All day long she flits from person to person, letting them admire her bruise. It's the exact shape of the wooden heel of Mrs. Webber's clog. It's purple and blue and heel-shaped.

When the final bell rings, however, she magically appears by my side.

"Hi," she says.

"Hi," I say.

She walks with me to the pickup lane outside the school.

"Do *you* want to touch my bruise?" she offers.

I do. I've wanted to all day long. But I say, "No, thanks."

"You don't? Why?"

I look her straight in the eyeballs, the way Mom wants me to do with Sandra and Winnie. Since I'm Lexie's sometimes best friend, I think she should have let me touch her bruise first, or at least in the first round of touching. Maybe she figured that since she was going home with me, I'd get one-on-one time with her bruise then. Maybe she figured I'd get more time with it than the other kids, so I didn't need time with it while we were at Trinity.

Maybe she's right, but it still hurts my feelings.

"I'm not allowed to touch other people's

bruises," I say. I stop looking at her eyeballs. "There's Sandra. Come on."

"Hmph," Lexie says.

On the way home, she chats with my sisters. She glances at me from time to time.

"Do you want to touch it now?" she whispers at a stoplight.

"No, thank you," I say in my regular voice. "But thanks for the offer."

"What offer?" Winnie says, craning around from the front passenger seat.

"Nothing!" Lexie says. She turns red and doesn't ask again.

When we get to my house, Winnie and Sandra go off to their rooms. Mom brings Baby Maggie downstairs and says "hi," but after putting out milk and cookies, she takes Maggie away again.

"It's her nap time," I tell Lexie.

"Your mom still takes naps?" Lexie says.

I start to say, *No, silly. Baby Maggie does.* Then I

realize Lexie *wants* me to say that. So I nod matter-of-factly and say, "Yep."

Lexie narrows her eyes.

I take another cookie from the plate on the kitchen table. "What do you want to do?"

"Something not boring," she replies.

"We could do our non-random acts of kindness. I could do a kindness for you, and you could do a kindness for me."

"I said *not* boring," Lexie says.

"But—" I close my mouth. I am in a mood of not liking her very much. I'm ready for her to go home, only she just got here. I can't complain to Mom, because all Mom would do is say, "Work it out."

"You choose something," I say to Lexie. "Something un-boring."

She smiles. It's a smile that makes me think of Mrs. Webber's egg timer, and like Mrs. Webber's egg timer, it gives me the shivers.

"The electric chair," she says smugly.

I put my head in my hands. Of course she picked the electric chair. She thinks it sounds so cool, when really it's just this stupid chair that goes up and down our back staircase. It's connected to a metal railing, and there's a button you press to make it work, and it's called the electric chair because it runs on electricity.

The lady who lived in this house before us was really old. That's why she had the electric chair. First she got so old that she couldn't climb stairs. Then she got so old that she died. She might have died *in* the electric chair—that's what my sisters say. They say our back staircase has ghosts.

"Well?" Lexie says.

I lift my head. "We're not allowed."

"Why?"

"Because it's too dangerous." I try to sound important. "It's too dangerous, and so Mom made a rule!"

"That's silly. I'll go ask your mom myself."

My hand snakes out, and I grab her forearm. "NO! I mean, no. She's, um. She's putting Maggie down for her nap. We aren't allowed to bother her."

Lexie looks at my hand on her arm. I let go.

"Hmm," she says. She sticks her legs out near me and crosses one foot over the other. She's wearing her cool black high-tops. The sparkly ones. "If the electric chair is so dangerous, why haven't your parents gotten rid of it?"

"Because . . . well—"

"I don't think there is a rule. I think you're just scared."

"Yeah, right. I'm *sooooo* scared." I make spooky hands. *"Oh no! It's a chair! Oh no, it's coming to get me!"*

She hops up from the kitchen table. "Then let's go, Mr. So Not Scared. Show me."

So, fine. I guess I have to. I mean, I can't think of any other plan . . . so I take draggy steps to the back staircase and do a limp flop with my arm.

"There," I say.

Her eyes get big. The electric chair is right in front of her on its steel railing. The cushion part is yellow-y and scratched, and so is the armrest, and she touches a peeling-off bit of fabric. It's old, just like Mrs. Robinson before she died.

On the bottom of the armrest is the power button, which you hold down to make the chair move. There's a power button on the wall, too, beneath the light switch. I don't know why there are two on/off buttons, unless Mrs. Robinson liked to ride the chair without doing any work at all? Maybe she'd perch on the chair like a queen while her husband or daughter or granddaughter pushed the button on the wall and sent her on her way.

Lexie's fingers scooch to the bottom of the armrest and hover above the power button. She pushes it, and the empty chair hums and lurches up the railing. Lexie squeals and lets go of the button. The chair stops. She laughs.

"*Who's* scared?" I say.

Her eyes are bright and her smile is brighter. "Not me," she says, going up one stair and climbing into the chair. She holds down the power button and giggles as the chair takes her up up up. "Adios, amigo!"

She looks like she's having fun, and there don't seem to be any ghosts. If there are, they're hiding. I almost decide I'm having fun, too, until I remember that I'm mad at her.

I push the power button on the wall, which maybe she doesn't even know about.

The chair stops.

She says, "Hey!"

"Ha-ha," I say.

I let go of the button, and because she's still pushing the button under the armrest, the chair lurches upward.

"*Hey!*" she cries.

"You did it, not me," I say.

She lets go of her button. The chair stops. I push down my button. The chair starts. She scowls and holds down *her* button, only mine is the boss button, because hers only works when I'm not pushing mine down and mine works no matter what.

So, even though she wants to stop the chair, the chair keeps going because I'm pressing the boss button. Ha-ha-ha.

"Ty, stop!" Lexie says.

"Bossy, bossy, bossy," I say, because I can.

"Ty! STOP!"

I keep pressing the button. She keeps going up. I smile.

She doesn't.

She hop-skaddles out of the chair *while it is moving*, and I am startled, but not startled enough—or maybe too startled—because I keep pressing the button.

The chair keeps going.

Lexie is in front of it.

Her leg is very very VERY in front of it, between the electric chair and the steel railing. Her foot is on the stair itself, which is BELOW the railing and the chair, and also BETWEEN the railing and the chair, and it is kind of like she—or her foot—is standing smack between two elevator doors that are closing, closing, closing. Only even so, the chair *still* keeps going.

She screams a scream, and it's bad. So bad there's even a word for it, and the word is *bloodcurdling*. Spiky cold things twist under my skin, and now I know. They are the curdles.

The chair jolts forward and rams Lexie's shin.

Her scream is the bloodcurdliest scream in the universe.

CHAPTER FOUR

I let go of the button, and the chair stops— *finally!*

But it's too late. Lexie's leg is pinned between the electric chair and the hard wooden stairs. Her foot in its black sparkly high-top is wedged between the edge of the stair and the motor of the chair. It is JAMMED IN. I can see it, and it is squished at the ankle between metal and wood. She tries to pull it out, but she can't.

"OW!" she bellows. "My leg, my leg, my-leg-my-leg!"

I've heard that sometimes time stands still, but I didn't think it was true. Or, I thought, *Okay, but not to me.*

Only, yes, it's true, and yes, to me. Lexie's leg is stuck, and so am I.

Then—*pop!* Time bubbles through and unfreezes me, and I sprint up the staircase and tug on Lexie's leg. No good.

Tears stream down her cheeks, and she is scared, I can tell, because her face is red and blotchy and her eyes are trying to jump out of her eyeball sockets.

"Hold on, it's okay," I say. I'm scared, too.

She reaches for her button, the on/off button beneath the arm of the chair, and I say, "No!"

She pushes it, and the chair jumps forward another half an inch ON TOP OF HER POOR SQUISHED LEG.

"Owwwww!" she cries.

"Don't do that!" I say. "You're just making it stuck-er!"

"Help!" she wails. "It *hurts!*"

"I know!"

"It *really* hurts!"

"I know, but—" I close my mouth. *But if you make the chair go forward any more, you'll break it,*

I was going to say. Meaning, her leg. *Snap.* But I keep that thought to myself.

"So," I say. "Um." My heart bam-bam-bams. I tug again on her leg.

"OW!" she shrieks.

"Sorry!"

I bite my lip and glance at the top of the staircase, wanting my mom and my sisters to come running, but also not wanting them to come running. I don't want to get in trouble. I do want Lexie to get unstuck.

No one comes running.

"You're doing a very good job of holding still," I tell Lexie, because she is, even with all the crying. "You're being very very brave."

"It hurts," she whimpers.

Then! A storm in my brain! A good one! I squat and flip the "change direction" lever on the motor of the chair. Why why *why* did I forget about the "change direction" lever? I stand back up and reach for the on/off button.

"No!" Lexie cries.

Too late again. I've already pressed it. But this time there's a happy ending, because with a creak and a groan, the chair goes *down* the staircase. *Down* the steel railing. *Down* away from Lexie's poor squished leg and poor trapped foot.

She's free! The disaster is *over*. PHEW.

It rains that night, and that's good. It's a good night for rain, especially since it's just rain and not thunder and lightning. It's a good night for hearing drumming sounds on the roof and for being snug inside with all the lights on and Parmesan chicken for dinner. I eat five pieces of French bread with butter, and Mom tells me I'm going to turn *into* French bread with butter, and what will she do with me then?

"Eat him up—yum!" Sandra says in a witchy voice, and I laugh with everyone else. The laugh that comes out isn't quite my laugh, but close enough.

Still.

Witches and trapped legs and a stormy night, even without thunder and lightning, make it hard for me to settle down. Lexie didn't tell on me when her mom came and picked her up, even though it was her fault for getting hurt since she was the one who wanted to play with the chair, but what if she decides to later? And when will Joseph ever come back? He's doing well. The doctors are always saying he's doing well. So why can't he just *be* well? Joseph never tells on me. He also never gets stuck in the electric chair.

Also, my recitation. I haven't done any of it. And a pet for Teensy Baby Maggie. I'm her big brother, and I made her a promise, and I need to keep it.

I'm actually ready for bed when Dad comes to tuck me in. Sometimes Dad tucks me in, and sometimes Mom, and there are pluses and minuses to both. But tonight it's Dad, and he's surprised to find me already in bed with the covers pulled up to my chin.

"Whoa," he says, sitting on the edge of the mattress. He lifts the covers. "You're already pajama-ed up. Good man."

I shrug.

"Did you brush your teeth?"

I huff at him—though I am *not* the Big Bad Wolf—and he sniffs my minty breath.

"Impressive," he says.

"Thanks."

"So what are we reading, partner? *Toy Dance Party* or *Lunch Lady and the Cyborg Substitute*?"

I sigh. Dad is the smartest man in the world, and I like his shirts that are nice and soft, even if the buttons sometimes dig in when he hugs me. He uses deodorant (I will, too, when I'm old), and it's called Axe. Mom tells him it makes him smell wonderful. I think it makes him smell safe. Maybe "wonderful" and "safe" are the same thing?

"Could we talk instead?" I say.

"Sure. What about?"

I look at him. I want to talk about Lexie. I want to tell him about the terrible thing that happened, but also how I fixed it, and how it ended up not being terrible after all. Just a red mark on Lexie's leg, and nowhere near as bad as the bruise on her head.

"Ty?" Dad says. "You all right?"

"I'm fine," I say. I reach for his hand, and he

wraps his fingers around mine. His skin is warm. "I have a friend—well, kind of a friend—and do you know what she told me?"

"What?"

"That she never gets in trouble, and that her parents never yell at her. And her name is Breezie. But I don't believe her. Do you?"

"That her name's Breezie, or that she never gets in trouble?"

"Ha-ha. Her name really is Breezie. But every kid gets in trouble sometimes, and every parent yells sometimes. Right?"

"Do I yell?" Dad asks.

"Well . . . no. But you have a stern voice, and you use that when I'm bad."

"Hold on," Dad says. "Have I ever told you you're *bad*, Ty?"

"Okay, not when I'm bad, but when I make bad decisions." I frown. "Do you think Breezie has never ever *ever* gotten in trouble, for real? Do you think her parents have never yelled at her *or* been stern with her?"

"Hmm. My guess is that every kid gets in trouble at some point, because nobody's perfect. And if a kid does get in trouble, I'd hope the kid's parents would make sure there was some kind of consequence. Otherwise, the parents wouldn't be helping the kid learn about right and wrong."

"What if the kid already knows right and wrong?"

"Sometimes it's a lesson that needs to be learned again and again, I'm sorry to say. Even for grown-ups."

So what happens when grown-ups mess up? I almost ask. *Who yells at them, or uses a stern voice, or makes sure they get a consequence?*

I decide not to, because out of nowhere an odd thought pops into my brain. Maybe, sometimes, a person can do a bad thing and *not* have to get in trouble. Maybe the person can learn the right and wrong part all by himself.

I feel lighter, as if an elephant had been sitting on my chest, but decided to get to its feet and lumber off.

"Okay," I tell Dad.

"Yeah? No more questions?"

"Just one. Can I get a puppy?"

"You cannot."

"I knew you would say that. How about a hyena?"

"No again."

"How about a platypus? How about if it's for Baby Maggie and not me?"

"And that's strike three. You are officially out." He flips off my light. "Love you, Ty."

"Love you, too, Dad."

He leaves, pulling my door halfway shut behind him because that's the way I like it. His feet go *bum bum bum* on the stairs. The rain goes *drum drum drum* on the roof. I stare at the glow-in-the-dark stars on my ceiling until my eyelids grow so heavy I can no longer keep them open. I drift off thinking a little about Lexie, and her cool high-tops, but also about getting older, and what I might be when I'm a grown-up. How, when I'm a dad, I'll say yes to getting a dog, but no to getting a hyena.

Probably.

CHAPTER FIVE

I wake up thinking about rainbows, and the reason why is because Sandra is shaking my shoulder and saying, "Ty! Wake up! There's a rainbow!"

"Huh?" I say. My bed is cozy, and my covers make a fort around me. I like it here.

But.

Sandra.

Sandra!

Sandra does not usually wake me up. Usually Sandra sleeps later than me, and when she *does* get up, she does girl things with makeup and her hairbrush and perfume that squirts out of a pretty glass bottle. She uses deodorant, too—like Dad—but hers is called Dove.

"Come look," Sandra says.

She grabs my wrist, and I slip out of bed and yawn as she leads me to my window. She kneels and puts her arm around me. She's opened the blinds already.

"See?" she says.

Outside, there are trees, and above the treetops is a pale blue sky. It shimmers the way new skies do. But where's the rainbow?

Sandra places her hands on the sides of my head and aims me to the right.

Ohhh. My heart swells. I know the colors by heart—red, orange, yellow, green, blue, indigo, violet—because Sandra taught me the "name" trick, which is Roy G. Biv. I can't tell the difference between indigo and violet, and also Winnie told me "indigo" got kicked out, but I don't care. I just like rainbows.

"I thought you'd like it," Sandra whispers, putting her arm around my shoulders and hugging me.

"I do," I whisper back.

It's a happy start to the day. It makes me feel . . .
well, like a bigger Ty than normal, and when I
get to school, I walk straight over to Lexie. My
stomach is jumpy.

"I have something to say," I tell her.

She stops coloring the numbers on the fake
money she's making. Lexie loves making fake
money. She cuts up construction paper and draws
her face in the middle and writes the number 5
on each corner, or 10 or 100. "I'm going to be
rich!" she likes to brag, and then she throws her
head back and laughs like a crazy, cackling rich
person.

So far, she just has a lot of fake money.

I move my weight from one foot to the other.
"I'm going to say it now—the thing I want to say.
But I don't want you getting wild. Okay?"

She doesn't look at me. She's probably mad

because of how our playdate ended yesterday, because it wasn't the greatest. I walked her to the door when her mom got there, because that's the rule. I said, "Thanks so much for coming," because that's the rule, too.

She didn't say, "Thanks so much for having me," though.

On the other hand, she also didn't tell on me for squishing her leg with the electric chair.

On the other *other* hand, I didn't tell on her for grabbing me around the neck and choking me once she was free from the chair. One minute I was standing on the stairs next to her, and the next minute—*bam!*—Lexie had me in a choke hold and wouldn't let go. I tried to pry her off, but Lexie is strong.

Then she added in the neck-pinch-of-death that Taylor taught us how to do during sharing time one day. He taught us step-by-step, because he knows karate. "I think that's enough of that,"

Mrs. Webber told him, but he kept talking even as she steered him back to his seat.

"The neck-pinch is a real karate move, people!" he said. "It can kill a three-hundred-pound man, and I mean it!"

And Lexie did the neck-pinch-of-death on me!

I said, "Stop!"

I said, "You are going to kill me!"

She kept doing it anyway. She did it for fifteen seconds, which was a close call, because I'm pretty sure it only takes thirty seconds before you're a goner. I yelled and yelled, and I was SO MAD when she let me go that I almost hit her.

I didn't, but I felt scared afterward. *Keep yourself safe, keep your friends safe, keep your school safe.* Those are the rules at Trinity, and I think they're good rules for everywhere. Like, instead of "school," you could say "house" or "swimming pool" or "park."

But Lexie didn't keep me safe, and I *almost* didn't keep her safe. Later, I realized I'd dug little moons into my palms with my fingernails. That's how hard I'd squeezed my fists.

Anyway, when her mom picked her up, she left the house without saying a word.

There are words I need to say now, though. I make myself say them before I chicken out.

"I'm sorry for yelling yesterday," I say.

She holds still. Even her shiny hair holds still. Lexie and Breezie both have shiny hair, but I like Lexie's better.

"I'm sorry for yelling, and that your leg got hurt, and . . . yeah." I feel stupid standing here. I think she should say sorry, too. She should at least say "apology accepted."

Instead, she goes back to coloring her fake

money. It makes me mad, but I don't *want* to be mad again.

"Well, that's all," I say, "except I think it was a good learning experience for both of us. Don't you?"

She doesn't nod or shake her head. She just keeps coloring her stupid money.

I walk away, but before I get to my desk, she says, "I'll check your loose tooth for you, if you want."

I pause. Last week, Taylor accidentally whammed me in the mouth with his elbow, and for a few days, I could wiggle my tooth with my tongue. For a few days, I thought, *Yay! Tooth fairy, here I come!* But my tooth doesn't seem nearly as loose anymore, so I guess my gums must have tightened up again.

I go back to Lexie. She pats the floor, and I drop to my knees.

"Open up," she says.

I do, and she wiggles the exact right tooth. She pulls her hand out of my mouth and wipes her fingers on her jeans.

"It's not even close," she says. "Sorry."

I slump.

"You could ask Taylor to hit you again," she suggests.

I glance at Taylor, who's stabbing holes in his reading folder with a pencil. His shirt says CRUNCHY.

"No thanks," I say.

"Or *I* could hit you," Lexie says, but before I even have time to frown, she says, "Kidding. Kidding! But at lunch, I'll find you a stick to bite on. Biting a stick will make it loose again."

"It will?"

"I'm pretty sure." She purses her lips, then picks up the ten-dollar bill she's made. No, it's a one-hundred-dollar bill, with Lexie's face smack-dab in the middle.

She flutters it at me. "Take it. Sheesh!"

It's a very good fake one-hundred-dollar bill. I transport it carefully to my desk and put it inside.

Then I remember my manners and go back and stand above her. "Um, thanks."

"Yeah-yeah, sure-sure," she says, hard at work on a new one. "Just don't spend it all in one place, kid."

CHAPTER SIX

After school, I go on errands with Mom and Baby Maggie. Mom calls it a "date" since it is kind of just the two of us, since Maggie doesn't talk yet and is still in her cute houseplant stage (except when she cries), but really it is just errands.

That's okay. I like the way the dry cleaner smells and how the lady pushes a button and *vroooom!* All the clothes on their hangers move closer like a giant centipede with swishy legs.

I like the bank because I like putting my elbows on the counter and JUMP-ing up so that my weight is on my forearms and my feet are dangling off the floor. The bank lady scowls at me—there is a sign that says PLEASE DO NOT

PUT YOUR CHILDREN ON THE COUNTER—but Mom doesn't make me get down, because *she* didn't put me there. I put me there myself. So, ha. I would rather not be scowled at, but I would also rather not stop dangling.

Our last stop of the afternoon is the mall, which is huge and filled with grown-up stores, and I'm worried Mom is going to want to go clothes shopping for herself. When she goes clothes shopping, it is b-o-r-i-n-g. I have to sit in the dressing room while she puts on clothes and takes off clothes and puts on clothes and takes off clothes. Sometimes there are fun-ish plastic tags on the floor to collect, and once I found a whole bunch of staples, but still. It's *not* a free-choice activity I'd ever pick.

"Mom, no shopping," I tell her when she pauses outside a window display. The mannequin is wearing a scarf. Scarves are dumb. "We're here to buy Dad a belt, remember?"

Dad has a work trip coming up. He needs a belt. I don't know why, except I guess to hold his pants up.

I pull her along three other times from clothes, one time from high heels, and one very firm time from the makeup area. "Mom, *no*," I say in my stern voice.

Then, after we buy Dad a brown belt, we pass a kids' shoe store. On a shelf-thing right inside the door is a pair of black high-tops, just like Lexie's, only better! Lexie's black high-tops are sparkly. These black high-tops have paint splattered all over them. White paint and red paint and green paint and blue paint, dribble-dribble-drop-drop over every inch of them!

"Mom!" I say, stopping dead still.

Mom, who is pushing Baby Maggie in her stroller, halts. She looks alarmed. "Ty?"

I grab her arm. I bend my knees and pull on her, and then I quit because she's told me how much she doesn't like it when I do that. So I *don't* pull on her, but I don't let go of her, and I say, "Mom-Mom-Mom, can I please get those shoes? Please-please-pretty-please? Because I need new shoes! And I am a growing boy! And those are really good shoes which will make me run faster and also have excellent posture, even though I am already the straightest-standing boy in my class, and yeah! Please? *Please?*"

She opens her mouth. She's about to say, "Sorry, Ty-bug, not today. We're not here to shop for you." I can tell she's about to say that, and I pull on her again—*oops*—and make a begging face and say, "PLEASE?!!"

She pushes her hand through her hair. She looks like she needs a nap. Teensy Baby Maggie's squeaky toy falls on the floor, and I dash and get it and hand it right back to Maggie, even though she doesn't even play with squeaky toys yet. I smile at Mom very cutely.

"Sure," she says.

My eyebrows fly up. "Really?"

"*If* they have them in your size, and *if* you don't ask for anything else. Deal?"

"Deal!" I say.

They do have them in my size, and they are *suh-weet*, and I wear them out of the store. I put my not-nearly-so-cool old shoes in the new shoes' box. I dance around Maggie's stroller.

"You just did a very non-random act of kindness," I tell Mom, feeling bouncy. "Thank you, thank you, thank you!"

"You're welcome," Mom says. "Take care of them. They were expensive for a seven-year-old's pair of sneakers."

"*High-tops*, Mom. And I will, and thank you again, and you don't have to buy me anything for a really long time."

"Hmm," Mom says.

"You don't. I mean it. Not for a whole month! Not until"—I think for a second—"August first! Okay?"

"This way, Ty," Mom says, and I jump and spin and follow her toward the end of the mall that connects to the parking garage. "And, for the record, August first is more than a month away. Much more."

"Wow," I say, impressed by how nice I am.

We pass the pet store, and I run over and press my forehead to the window, cupping my hands around

my face. "Mom!" I say. "Can I get a snake? Please? I will be the one to take care of it, I promise!"

"No," Mom says.

"A ferret? Can I get a ferret? Look how fluffy they are!"

"No ferrets, no snakes, no pets *at all*," Mom says.

"But—"

"I thought you weren't going to ask for anything until August first."

Oh, I think. *Poop.*

At home, I discover something bad. Actually, I discovered it in the parking lot of the mall, but I couldn't *do* anything about it until now. And here is the something bad: My new shoes are too big! I thought they fit at the store. I really did. But suddenly they don't!

There's NO WAY I'm telling Mom, though. Instead, I put on a bonus pair of socks, and guess what? Now they (almost) fit perfectly! They still hurt a little because of slip-sliding on my heels and maybe making blisters, but I'm tough. I will deal with it, and my feet will grow, and . . . yeah.

In the kitchen, while Mom fixes dinner, I do jumps and kicks around the table. I add in karate chops and karate noises, too. *Kai-yah! Cha-cha-cha! KER-PLAM!*

"Ty," Mom says.

"I'm protecting you!" I say.

"I don't need protecting. I do, however, need someone to set the table. Would you set the table, please?"

"I'll protect Baby Maggie, then," I say. It's the least I can do since I wasn't able to buy her a ferret or an ocelot. (Since SOMEONE didn't let me.)

Mom shoots me a look.

"I'll set the table, too," I quickly promise.

But first, I do a twirl-about with a flying lunge.

"Flak-schweeky!" I cry, flinging out my arms to block Baby Maggie from flying aliens or escaped mushrooms.

Baby Maggie blinks.

I thrust my right arm into the air and do wiggle fingers. My feet go dance-dance-dance, and I say, "Yeah!"

Baby Maggie gurgles and does her own wiggle fingers. She lifts her chubby legs and does wiggle feet, too.

"Ty," Mom says.

"All right, all right," I say. In my head, I add, *Hold yer horses, lady.* I'll do one more move, and then I'll set the table.

For my finale, I do a super-duper double high kick and plop one of my super-duper new high-tops on the granite counter by the stove.

"Boom!" I proclaim, spreading my arms wide. I bounce a little on my other foot for balance.

"TY! Get your foot off the counter!" Mom yells.

I jump. I lose my balance and fall backward and land on the floor.

"Mom, you scared me!" I say. Then I smile and give her a thumbs-up. "Good one!"

Teensy Baby Maggie blows a spit bubble and throws up. It's awesome.

CHAPTER SEVEN

On Thursday, Mom tells me I can't get a hedgehog or a jackalope or even an armadillo.

"Pooey," I say. I eat a bite of toast and drink the last of my orange juice. "Can I have more juice, please, and how about a camel? If we got a camel, we wouldn't even need a litter box, because camels hardly ever pee."

"Yes to the juice, no to the camel," Dad says, jumping into the conversation. He hasn't left for work yet. He refills my glass, and then he refills Winnie's glass. Teensy Baby Maggie is in her bouncy seat on top of the table, and Dad pretends to refill her juice, too. But Baby Maggie doesn't even have a juice glass. Silly Dad.

"We don't need any more pets, bud," he tells me. "We've got Sweetie-Pie."

"Why does everyone keep saying that?" I complain.

"Because it's true," Sandra says, strolling over to the table and swiping what's left of my toast from my plate. "Also, we've got *you*."

"Hey!" I say.

"Hey what?" she says. "You don't like crusts."

"'Hey' I'm not your pet," I say. To Dad I say, "And Sweetie-Pie belongs to Winnie. Why does Winnie get a pet, but not me or Sandra or Baby Maggie?"

"Because no one else *wants* a pet," Sandra says in her normal voice. In my ear, she says, "And like I said, I've already got y-o-u."

Her breath tickles. I push her away.

"Baby Maggie does so want one," I say. "She told me in secret baby language. So how about a mouse? A mouse would be no trouble *at all*. I promise."

"Yeah, because Sweetie-Pie would eat it," Sandra says.

"Sandra!" Winnie protests. "Sweetie-Pie would not eat a sweet little mouse!"

"What if it was mouse pie?" Sandra says.

"It wouldn't be," Winnie says. "It would be a plain old mouse. Right, Ty?"

"What if Mom cooked it? What if Mom cooked it by accident?" Sandra says.

"Not a plain old mouse. A cute mouse," I say.

"Like a rat, you mean?" Sandra says. She leans back in her chair. "Hey, Mom, would you make rat pie if Ty got a rat?"

"I would not," Mom says from the sink, where she's washing dishes.

"Ellen, let me do that," Dad says, stepping behind her and taking the pan from her hands. "And kids, enough. Ty? No pets. Sandra? No pie."

"Not even boysenberry?" Sandra says.

"Poison berry!" Winnie says. She puts her hand to her heart.

"No poison berry," Dad says. "And all of you, listen up. I want you to help your mom out tonight. I have to stay late at the office, so she'll be on her own."

Mom pushes her hair off her forehead with the back of her hand. "Alone?" she mutters. "Hardly." When she realizes that I heard that, she smiles. "We'll be fine. We'll have fun." Her tired look comes back. "I just have to figure out something for dinner."

"Mouse pizza!" Sandra cries.

"Poison pizza!" Winnie cries. Then, "*Kidding*, Dad."

In her bouncy seat, Teensy Baby Maggie waves a fist in the air. She kicks her foot. Her sock is half off. It always is, except when it's all the way off.

"Oh, and Ty," Mom says. "I can't believe I haven't told you . . ."

"Told me what? That it's a yes to the jackalope?" I thrust my arms into the air. "You are the best mommy ever!"

"No, Ty, it's—"

I get up and shake my booty. "Wh-hoo! A jack-alope!"

Winnie laughs.

I fling my arms around Mom's waist and talk on top of her. "Best! Mommy! Ever! Thank you, my bestest mommy!"

"Hmm," Sandra says, making a thinking face. "A jackalope will change the family dynamic, sure, but . . . oh, what the heck. I suppose I can get behind a jackalope."

"And get kicked?" Dad says.

"Huh?"

"Jackalopes also have strong legs. If you stand behind one—"

"Hardy har har," Sandra says.

"*My* jackalope won't be the kicking kind," I say into Mom's stomach.

"True, because your jackalope will be the invisible kind," Mom says.

"Oh, Mother, I am so disappointed in you," Winnie says.

I grin at her, because she's funny. That's why she's my favorite sister.

Except Sandra showed me the rainbow, so sometimes Sandra's my favorite sister. And Teensy Baby Maggie is so cute! And so are her teensy baby socks! I tried to make ear mittens out of them once, but they fell right off.

You're my favorite sister, too, I tell Baby Maggie, using my brain power. *And I'm working VERY HARD on getting you a pet, and I promise it won't be a boring invisible jackalope. You can count on me, bitsy Mags!*

Mom pushes me off of her.

"Ty?" she says.

I lock my eyeballs with hers. "Yes, my mommy?"

"I have terrific news—and please don't interrupt."

"When do I interrupt? I never interrupt!"

Mom arches her eyebrows.

Sandra snort-laughs.

"Joseph's coming home," Mom says.

The world stops.

I don't breathe.

Then Winnie draws her hands to her mouth, and Baby Maggie kicks her leg, and her sock flies off her foot and onto my plate.

"When?" I whisper.

"Hopefully this weekend," Mom says. "He is ready to leave the hospital, and as long as he doesn't get a last-minute cold . . ." She takes my hands. "Pretty awesome, huh?"

I feel funny. I think it's because I'm breathing in a funny way. Like, in and out and in and out, but more quickly than normal. Like, if I were blowing up a balloon, I'd be unblowing it at the exact same time.

I want Joseph to come home. I want him to come home so much it hurts.

But . . .

"How would he get a last-minute cold?" I say.

"Oh, baby, he won't," Mom says.

"What *is* a last-minute cold?" I say.

Mom ruffles my hair. "Forget I said that. There's no need for you to worry."

"Ty always worries," Winnie says.

Maybe Mom sees how fast my chest is going up and down, because she says, "Baby. Sweetheart, please."

My brain thinks bad thoughts. Flying clogs, dead flies, last-minute colds. Lexie's howl when her leg was trapped by the electric chair. Joseph's hospital bed, which is fun to play on—and I should know, because I've played on it tons. But real beds are better. House beds, even if they don't move when you push a button.

"Dude," Sandra says. She leans toward me, tilting her chair onto its back legs even though it's against the law. She snaps her fingers in my face.

I blink.

"Does Joseph have a cold right now?" she asks.

I glance at Mom, who shakes her head.

"No," I say.

"What about you? Do *you* have a cold right now?"

I start to answer.

She talks on top of me. "Or, wait, let me put it this way. Has your leg fallen off this morning?"

What she's asking is just plain goofy, but I lift one leg and wiggle it. "No."

"And your head. Has your head rolled off your neck and gone bouncing across the floor?"

I try to lift my head off my neck, but it's on good and tight.

Mom shoots Dad a look.

Dad shrugs.

"Just as I suspected," Sandra says. She bangs her chair down, and the shock wave makes Teensy Baby Maggie's arms and legs flail.

We all laugh, and laughing makes my chest

loosen. We're not laughing *at* baby Maggie, though. She just looks so cute. She waves her arms and legs some more, like a blobby sea creature in pink pajamas.

"Sorry, Mags," Sandra says. "But do you see, Ty?"

"Do I see what?"

"This!" Sandra says, pushing lightly on Maggie's rib cage and making her bounce in her bouncy seat.

"I agree," Winnie says.

"With *what*?" I say.

"Yes, girls," Mom says. "With what?"

Winnie shrugs. "Well, you can't worry about the past, and you can't worry about the future. Or rather, you can, but what good would it do?"

"You have to live in the now," Sandra says. "Like Maggie."

"Yeah, because she doesn't know how *not* to," Winnie says.

They look at me. Everyone in the room looks at me, except for Maggie. Maggie's more interested in the ceiling.

I want to make them happy, so I say, "Maggie lives . . . in the now?"

Winnie's expression softens. "Yeah, because Maggie doesn't worry about anything. She just *lives.*"

"Exactly," Sandra says. "This little bitsy"—she gestures at Maggie—"she *is* life. Okay?"

"Ohhhh," I say, even though I have no idea what they're talking about. I wave at Baby Maggie. "Hi, life."

CHAPTER EIGHT

At school, I give Lexie a thousand-dollar bill I made. Instead of Lexie's head in the middle, I put a picture of Cyber Grape, who is big and purple. I invented him.

Lexie says, "Thanks," and in my maniac voice, I say, "You're welcome," which makes Lexie laugh. My maniac voice always makes her laugh.

Then Taylor comes over and says that I'm *in love* with Lexie, WHICH I AM NOT.

But when I say, *"No,"* he says, "Yes you are, because you're blushing!"

"No!" I say again. "I've been doing my maniac voice. *That's* why I'm blushing."

"You admitted it!" Taylor crows. He dances

around and points at me. "You admitted you're blushing! Ha-ha!"

I scowl. I'm mad at myself for saying the word "blushing," because I should have said, "And my face gets red when I do my maniac voice, that's all." I'm also mad at Mrs. Webber for leaving the classroom to get more construction paper. Taylor always acts up when she's gone.

"Ty lo-oves Lexie!" Taylor chants. "Ty lo-oves Lexie!"

"I don't," I tell Taylor.

I look at Lexie, who's clutching Breezie's arm and giggling.

"I *don't*," I tell Lexie, and I think about how lucky Teensy Baby Maggie is. She's too young for crushes and teasing and being danced around by annoying Taylor.

Sandra and Winnie said I should be more like Maggie, because Maggie waves her arms and legs and doesn't worry about things. But when Maggie is seven, will she still wave her arms and legs and not worry about things?

If she does, people will think she is extremely strange.

Taylor skip-hops over to me. "Say you love Lexie. Say it, or I'm going to do the neck-pinch on you!"

"Do it!" Lexie cries. "Do it, do it!"

Does she want Taylor to do the neck-pinch on me, or me to say I love her?

I don't want either to happen. I clench my hands

into fists and say, "Taylor? This is why you don't
have any friends! Because you're being bully-ish,
that's why!"

Taylor stops in his tracks. His hyperness
whooshes out of him. He grows smaller, *right in
front of my eyes*, and a huge rubber band squeezes
my chest because I know I said something mean.

I'm still hot. I'm still mad. But I feel horrible,
too, because *I* was just a bully. *Me*. Not with my
fists, but with my words. If someone said "this is
why you don't have any friends" to Teensy Baby
Maggie, she would cry.

"Yeah, Taylor," Hannah says. "I've told you that
so many times. If you want people to be nice to
you, you have to be nice to them."

"Like bringing doughnuts for the whole class,"
Chase says.

"Only not the cake kind," Elizabeth says.

"Or the ones with nuts on top," John says.

"The glazed ones," Elizabeth says. "Those are

the best. But Ty, *are* you in love with Lexie? And Lexie, are *you* in love with Ty?"

"No!" cries Lexie.

"Are you sure?" Chase says. "Because look— now *Lexie's* blushing!"

Then everyone talks at the same time, words words words, and most of them fighting-ish. Elizabeth goes to Lexie and Breezie, and Breezie pushes Elizabeth away. Hannah gets in Chase's face. Chase sneezes on her, and I think it's on purpose. John says that *some* cake doughnuts are good, and Elizabeth says, "Ew! You are so gross!"

"People!" I say. I glance anxiously at the door. I glance anxiously at Taylor, only he's still deflated, so no more looking at that deflated boy.

I raise my voice. "*People!* Mrs. Webber is coming!"

Everyone shuts up. There are three seconds of silence, or possibly four, but no one hears Mrs. Webber coming down the hall.

"Wrong!" Hannah calls, and all the noise starts up again. Hannah talks over it. "And Chase? If you have *germs*, and you sneezed them into my *mouth*—"

"Crushes are stupid. But if I *did* have a crush on anyone—"

"What about *blueberry* cake doughnuts?"

It's a madhouse. It's a madhouse without Mrs. Webber, and it's a madhouse even *with* Mrs. Webber, when she finally comes back into the room.

"Class!" she barks.

We clam up for real. Well, I've already clammed up. Taylor, too. But the other kids clam up with us and freeze where they are.

Mrs. Webber lectures us. She reminds us of Trinity's rules, and she makes us recite them: *Keep yourself safe. Keep your friends safe. Keep your school safe.*

"All right?" she says.

We nod.

"Good. Now I want you all to—"

Taylor raises his hand.

Mrs. Webber presses her fingers to the spot between her eyebrows.

Taylor waggles his hand. He waggles it harder. He waves his entire arm back and forth like he's an airport worker guiding in an airplane.

Is he going to tell Mrs. Webber what I said to him? I feel sweaty, so when Mrs. Webber closes her eyes, I step toward him and whisper, "I'm sorry I said you don't have friends."

Taylor keeps his hand in the air.

"And you are *sometimes* bully-ish, but not always." I take a breath. "And I was mean to say that, so . . . I'm sorry."

Taylor's hand drops an inch or two, like a kite. "Really?"

I nod. I don't want to be Taylor's best friend, and I don't want to invite him over to my house. But I *am* sorry for making him feel bad.

"Okay," Taylor says, and he puts his hand all the way down. Just like that.

Mrs. Webber opens her eyes, and—just like that—Taylor jams his hand up again.

"Ooo! Ooo!" he says. "Pick me!"

"Yes, Taylor?" Mrs. Webber says, sounding as tired as Mom sometimes sounds.

"How about mooning?" he asks. "Do you know what mooning is? It's when someone flashes you with his bottom. Want me to show you?"

Everyone laughs, or almost everybody. Breezie might not. But I do, because it's just like Taylor to ask about *mooning*.

"No, Taylor, I do not want you to show me," Mrs. Webber says. "Keeping your school safe includes keeping your teachers safe, and you need to keep me safe from that sight."

"But—"

"I don't want to see your bottom."

"But—"

"End. Of. Story," Mrs. Webber says. "And when

I say 'end,' I am referring to *your* end, Taylor. So zip it."

Lots of people laugh, and after school, when I tell Mom all about it, *she* laughs.

"He's such a rascal," I tell her, meaning Taylor. "He asks inappropriate questions—like about mooning—all the time. Like, one per second."

"Goodness," Mom says. We're sitting side by side on the sofa. She rubs her fingernails up and down my arm the way I like. "I'm glad you don't do that."

"I don't," I say. "But Taylor isn't *bad*. He just makes bad decisions."

"That's right," Mom says. "I'm proud of you for saying that, Ty-bug."

I feel happy, and I say, "Do you think you should buy me a koala bear to say 'yay' for being such a good boy?" I ask. "Koala bears eat leaves, and if we had one, I'd eat leaves, too. Like salad. Wouldn't that be great, Mom?"

"Interesting proposition, but no," she says.

I exhale. Thinking about Baby Maggie helped me at school today, and I want to do something to tell Maggie thank you.

"I could make you a snack, though," Mom says. "How about a delicious salad? You could pretend to be a koala bear."

I look at her. My look says, *Really, lady? Really?*

"Cookies and milk it is," Mom pronounces, kissing the top of my head.

She stands and heads for the kitchen. I consider following her to make sure she doesn't do the delicious salad thing, but at the last second, I change my mind.

I check to make sure I'm alone, and then I scooch like an inchworm until I'm lying on my back on the sofa. I lift my arms and legs. I wiggle them all around.

"*Bah,*" I say. "*Bah-bah goo-goo-gah.*"

I think Baby Maggie's onto something.

CHAPTER NINE

I have a problem. A huge problem.

I go find Winnie, who's lying on her bed and typing on her laptop. She's bobbing her head, which is connected by a pink cord to her computer.

I stand in front of her and say, "Hey! You in the unicorn shirt—I need your help!"

She takes out her earbuds. "Huh?" she says.

"I have a recitation tomorrow, and you have to help me. Please?"

"Recitations!" she says. "I remember those. Does everyone still end with 'Any comments or questions?'"

"Uh-huh, but that's the easy part. The hard part is that I have to give a speech. I'm supposed to do an act of kindness, and that's what the speech is supposed to be about."

"Can't Mom help you?"

"She's busy, and anyway, we're not supposed to bug her because Dad's coming home late and she has to deal with us all on her own. Remember?"

"Ah. Right." Winnie studies me, then says, "One sec. Let me tell Cinnamon and Dinah I'll be back."

Cinnamon and Dinah are Winnie's best friends. I try to be patient while she types some more, but as soon as she closes her laptop, I plop down on her bed beside her.

"*And* I promised Maggie I'd get her a pet," I say, diving right in. "Mom says she doesn't need a pet, but even so, I want to be a man of my word."

Now that Winnie is listening, my mind starts going way too fast, because there is so much trapped inside me. Like about Lexie and Breezie and Taylor. Like the neck-pinch-of-death. Like how Joseph will be coming home soon—*yay!* But only if he doesn't get a cold—*boo.*

I want to tell Winnie all these things, but before I can, my thoughts loop right back to where I started: No pet for Maggie, no pet for Maggie. No act of kindness, either.

Aaagh. I press the heels of my palms into my eyeball sockets.

"What's wrong?" Winnie says.

"Everything! I haven't done my recitation, and it's due tomorrow. Also, I keep thinking about things I don't want to think about, and plus it's been a crazy week. That's what's wrong. It's been a crazy, crazy, *crazy* week!"

"How so?" Winnie asks.

I open my mouth. I shut it. I *want* to tell her, but my words are stuck in molasses.

"Just tell me," Winnie says. "It'll make you feel better. I promise."

I hold my breath for a few seconds. Then,

loudly, I let it out. "Well . . . it all started when Mrs. Webber whacked Lexie in the head with her clog."

"Exsqueeze me?"

"No! Wait! Because *before* that, Sandra said how we don't need any more pets because of Sweetie-Pie, and Dad said that same thing, too. But Sweetie-Pie is *your* cat, right?"

"Whoa, go back. Mrs. Webber whacked Lexie with her clog?"

"Uh-huh, her wooden clog. EXCEPT WAIT AGAIN, BECAUSE ALSO LEXIE GOT HER LEG TRAPPED!"

"She got her leg trapped *and* she got whacked by a clog?!"

My gut clenches. I should have been more careful. I should have remembered not to share the "trapped" part.

"But she's *fine*," I hurry to say. "She doesn't have a limp or anything!"

"Ty?" Winnie says politely.

"Yes?"

"Please explain."

"Explain what?"

"Everything. *Now.*"

I gulp and do as she says. I talk and talk and *talk.*

When I get to the end, I notice something strange. I pat my chest, and then I pat my shoulders and the tops of my arms. Once I'm sure of what my body's telling me, I say, "Huh. I *do* feel better! I don't feel like I'm being flattened by an anvil anymore."

"Mmm," Winnie says. It's more of a rumble than a word, but she doesn't flick me or roll me off her bed or tell me to leave, so . . .

"Thanks, Winnie," I say.

"You're welcome," she says.

"And *you're* welcome for saying 'you're welcome,'" I say. "Now, can we focus here? We have a recitation to write!"

"We?"

"Yes, we! I'm so glad we agree. And now I will build us a rabbit hutch so we can think better."

I have to push Winnie to the side so that I can get to her pillow, because I need all the pillows I can find. I arrange them the way I want to make the walls of our hutch, and I prop them up using Winnie's sheets and blankets. When I've made a tight square, I pull Winnie's comforter over the whole caboodle. The comforter is the roof *and* the front door flap. Oh, and I don't know why Winnie and I call this kind of fort a rabbit hutch. We just do.

"Come on in," I say to Winnie, wiggling to the back and holding the door flap open. As Winnie crawls in, I ask, "Do you think Mom would let me get a cute little rabbit? And it could hop cutely through the house and sleep in my bed?"

"No," Winnie says. "Anyway, I thought the point was to get a pet for Maggie, not you."

"I know. I'm just saying the rabbit *could* sleep with me, because Maggie might squish it."

"Maggie doesn't even roll over yet. How would Maggie squish it?"

"Her blankie could squish it. And rabbits are so cute! And we could name it Little Bunny Foo Foo—or Pinkie, because bunnies have pink noses, and Baby Maggie loves pink!"

"Oh? How do you know?"

"Because all girls love pink. Geez, Winnie."

"Um, no. Some do, some don't. *Geez*, Ty."

"Whatever," I say. It's cozy and safe in our rabbit hutch. The rest of the world is good, too, but it's nice to take a break from all that bigness.

I cuddle up to Winnie and think about things. I think about tomorrow, when Mrs. Webber will say, "Your turn, Ty," and everyone will stare at me and wait for me to come to the front of the room.

"I guess I'll have to drop out of school," I say. "I'll have to be homeschooled, I guess." I sigh. "We don't even have a playground, *or* a water fountain."

"Ty, you're adorable," Winnie says. "You are also ridiculous. You're going to drop out of school *why*? Because you don't know what to do for your recitation?"

"Uh-huh."

"But you've done a gazillion acts of kindness this week. Just pick one and write about it."

"A *gazillion* acts of kindness?" I say. "I haven't done a *single* act of kindness! Not one!"

"Hmm," she says. "Let's review, shall we? After Mrs. Webber clobbered Lexie with her clog, who went and got Mrs. Jacobs?"

"Um . . . me?"

"Yup, and when Lexie had to leave early and almost left her shoes, who grabbed them for her?"

"M-me?"

"Exactly, and stop sounding so tentative— which means uncertain. It *was* you. You, you, you." She leans back and puts her feet in my lap. "And there's more. Who told Breezie not to worry and that Lexie wouldn't end up with a dent?"

"Me," I say. Because she's right. I did.

"Who saved the fly from being eaten or having its wings torn off?"

"Me!"

"Who didn't tell on Lexie for doing the deadly neck-pinch on you?"

"Me again!"

"And how about this one: Who didn't punch Lexie in the face even though he wanted to, and who even apologized for the whole bad playdate thing?"

"*Me*, and also I made her fake money with a picture of Cyber-Grape in the middle."

"*And* you're a good friend to Joseph, *and* you'll help him out when he returns to school, which hopefully will be next week."

"Yes, but I can't do my recitation about something that hasn't happened yet."

"Says who?"

"Says . . . I don't know! The President of Obama!"

A rain cloud sneaks into our rabbit hutch and turns everything gray again. For a millisecond, Winnie's list had made me feel better. Now it all falls apart. "And, Winnie. All those things you said I did?"

"All of those things you *did* do," she says, jabbing me with her toe.

"None of them was on purpose," I say.

"So?"

"So how can I give a speech about an act of kindness that was secretly just an accident?"

"*Were* they accidents?" Winnie asks. "Or were they just you being you?"

My heart is lumpish in my chest. I don't see how there's a difference, really.

"You, Ty, are a kind person," Winnie says. "Deal with it. But if you're going to sit there and be all mopey, then do something about it."

"Like what?" I say.

"Like . . . like pick someone in our family and do an on-purpose act of kindness. It's not that complicated."

I think about that. Then I think about puppies. Puppies and kittens and little mousies!

Winnie does her mind-reading trick and shakes her head. "No, sir," she says. "You can't do your kindness for Baby Maggie, because getting her a pet isn't going to happen. Not tonight."

"But—"

"Put that one on hold. And not to be a party pooper, but don't act-of-kindness me, either. I've enjoyed our time together, but all good things come to an end."

Hmmph, I think. She just wants to get back to

chatting with Cinnamon and Dinah on her computer.

"You could try Sandra," Winnie suggests.

"Sandra?" I say. "And do *what*?" The only kindness Sandra would want would be for me to leave her alone.

Winnie makes a sound low in her throat, because she knows I'm right. She scrunches her forehead. "Well, who's the only other person left? *Mom.* And who needs help tonight, anyway?"

"Mom!" I say "Because Dad's doing his late thing!"

"Exactamundo!"

We high-five each other in the rabbit hutch. One of the walls falls down.

"So there you have it," Winnie says. "Imagine your husband's staying late at work, and you're worn out, and you have a baby who you love, but who sometimes cries . . ."

"I don't have a husband or a baby."

"Imagine, I said. Imagine all that and then

come up with something kind to do for Mom. Easy-peasy pudding-and-pie!"

Easy-peasy pudding-and-pie, huh? Well . . . I *am* good at imagining stuff. I'm also good at winking each of my eyes separately, plus I can wink them one after the other, rapid-fire like *wink wink wink*. Winnie calls me a winking fool.

Winking at Mom wouldn't count as an act of kindness, though. She might even say *"Ty"* that way she does sometimes, like I'm wearing her out.

So, okay, what *wouldn't* wear her out? What would make her smile and put her in a good mood for the whole entire night?

I do my air of wisdom to help me think, which means tilting my head and stroking my beard.

Winnie breaks down the rest of the rabbit hutch. She says, "Good-bye, Ty. Go do your air of wisdom somewhere else."

But I don't need to, because I've got it!

I scramble off Winnie's bed and make a bee-line for the kitchen. Humming, I get to work.

CHAPTER TEN

O n Friday morning, Mrs. Webber doesn't wear her wooden clogs. This is her non-random act of kindness, I think, even though she doesn't say so.

We sit on the carpet for morning meeting, and Mrs. Webber tells us the good news about Joseph coming back to school. I already know, but I don't act braggy. I just grin and say "yay" with everyone else.

"Will he still be bald?" Taylor asks.

Joseph is a temporary baldie because of being sick. Because of the medicines and stuff the doctors gave him for his leukemia. Except he must not need them anymore if he's coming back to school!

"He will," Mrs. Webber says. "His hair will grow back eventually, but—"

"Will he wear his red woolly hat?" Elizabeth asks.

"I don't know. I suppose we'll find out," Mrs. Webber says. "I do know that he'll still need to be careful about germs—"

"Like having that bottle of hand sanitizer on his desk all the time," Lexie says.

"Yes," Mrs. Webber says. "And we'll all need to be careful about helping him stay healthy."

"Like not sneezing on him," Taylor says. He turns to Chase. "Ka-CHOO!" he says, sneezing a pretend sneeze all over him.

"Thank you, Taylor," Mrs. Webber says, giving him a look. "Thank you for showing the class what *not* to do." Then she claps her hands, a single clap that says it's time to move on. "Now, I know you've all worked hard on your recitations," she says. "Who wants to go first?"

Lexie's hand flies into the air like a rocket. She

waves it around and bounces on her bottom. Taylor jams his hand into the air, too. He adds in what he always adds in, which is, "Ooo! Ooo! Pick me, pick me!"

Mrs. Webber does what she always does, which is to pick someone with a raised hand who isn't doing any waving, bottom-bouncing, or *ooo*-ing.

"I like how Hannah is raising her hand so politely," she says. "Hannah? Would you like to come to the front of the room?"

Hannah does—and she brings doughnuts! In a box! She passes the box around, and I choose a maple-glazed one. Yummy!

She makes her speech, and she calls on me when it's time for comments or questions.

I say, "My comment is thank you very much, and also I like your shirt."

She glances at her shirt, which has a gold star in the middle of it.

"Okay," Hannah says.

She calls on a few more kids for comments and questions.

Then it's time for the next kid to give his recitation, and that kid is me. I stand up. I go to the front of the class. I face everyone and clear my throat.

Lexie giggles, and I almost giggle, too. But I stuff that giggle down because Mrs. Webber likes us to be serious during recitations.

I shake out my piece of paper, and Lexie giggles again. Maybe because I remind her of Abraham Lincoln? Because I'm being *so* serious?

I ignore that girl and read my speech aloud:

"Last night, my dad wasn't home. That meant my mom was the only one around to take care of us, and she's always really tired because of our new baby."

"Teensy Baby Maggie!" Lexie calls out. "Who is also bald, like Joseph!"

"Lexie, shush," Mrs. Webber says. "Ty, please go on."

I have to find my place. "Um . . . um . . . Mom's *also* the only one who takes care of us in the mornings, usually. And she's never able to eat breakfast because she's too busy running around. So last night, I didn't want that same thing to happen, and so guess what? I made dinner for the whole family. I did it sneakily, while my mom wasn't in the kitchen, and I made sure it was healthy, too."

I take a breath.

"It made me feel happy inside, and it made my mom feel full of food. It also made her kinder, because she was less frustrated."

I glance at the class to see if they're impressed. They are. *Good.*

I look back at my paper. "She told me, 'Ty, thank you so much. That was a huge help.' Also, she let us watch one family TV show, even though it was eight o'clock! And I told my mom that I would fix dinner the next night, too, and every night from now until infinity, or until I move out of the house. The end."

I let the hand which is holding my paper fall to my side. "Any comments or questions? Yes, Taylor?"

"What did you make?"

"For dinner?" I say. "Graham crackers with peanut butter, mini-marshmallows, and raisins. For drinks, everyone got to choose between orange juice, milk, or water. Oh, and I used fancy glasses."

"What about dessert?" Taylor asks.

I answer quickly, because after a recitation, you're only allowed to call on three people for comments or questions. I don't want Mrs. Webber to think Taylor is my number one *and* my number two person.

"More mini-marshmallows," I say.

I move on to the next question. "Yes, Mrs. Webber?"

"What did your mom say when you volunteered to make dinner every night from now on?" she asks.

"That we'll play it by ear, but what a nice offer."

"Ah," Mrs. Webber says. "Smart woman."

"Uh-huh." I only get to pick one more person, but even so, almost everyone has his or her hand up. But friends are supposed to pick friends, so I call on Lexie.

Lexie sits up straighter. "I thought you were going to get a pet for your baby sister, Maggie. What happened to getting her a pet?"

"I still will," I say. "Because during dinner we talked about that! And my sister Winnie reminded my mom that when *she* was a kid, my dad said that if she could catch a bird, she could keep it."

"A *bird* bird?" Lexie says. "Like, from a tree?"

"Oh my," Mrs. Webber murmurs.

"And so Winnie asked if the same was true for me, and my mom said, 'Well, your father made that deal. Not me.' But we said, 'Only you're the parent in charge, since Dad isn't here. *Sooooo?*'"

Even Breezie is leaning forward out of curiousness. "What did she say?"

"She said, 'Oh, good heavens,'" I tell Breezie. "And then she said, '*Fine.* If you can actually catch a bird, Ty, then sure. You can keep it.'"

"Ha," Breezie says. "Because she knows you can't."

"Except I feel very certain in my bones that I can," I say.

I think that birds are nice, and that baby Maggie will love hers very much once I catch it. I also think that Joseph and I will probably do the catching together, since Mom never said I wasn't allowed to have help.

"Well, do report back," Mrs. Webber says. Her expression suggests that she's wondering how smart Mom is after all.

I know that Mom is supersmart, and I could clear up that confusion for Mrs. Webber if I wanted to.

Instead, I salute and say, "Will do."

READ THE FIRST BOOK STARRING TY!

READ THE NEXT BOOK STARRING TY!

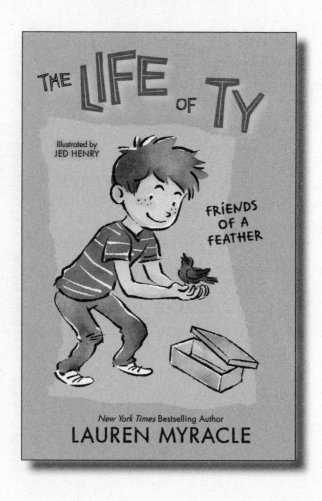